# THEA OF OZ

## Book One of the Ozite Cycle

Rebecca A. Demarest

Illustrated by Jason Morgado

WRITERLY BLISS

Boston

Writerly Bliss Publishing
http://rebeccaademarest.com

The characters and events in this book are fictitious. Any similarity to real persons, living or dead, is coincidental and not intended by the author.

*Book Design by Rebecca Demarest*

The fonts in this book include:

**Grantham, Imperator** and BIRMINGHAM by Paul Lloyd

*Palatino Linotype* by Hermann Zapf

Printed in the United States of America by createspace.com

# THEA OF OZ

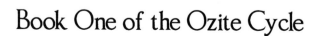

Book One of the Ozite Cycle

# 1

I took my time arranging the chipped tea service on the silver tray, trading one particularly well-loved cup for one less worse-for-wear. It wasn't like Auntie couldn't afford to buy a new set here in Oz, but these were Earth-made and Auntie was nothing if not Earth-proud. It was how she made her living, but when high-profile guests stopped by, it would have been nice to have something to serve them with that was whole, and maybe even matched. Nudging one last pastry into place, I grabbed the tray and backed through the swinging door into the living room.

"Elphred, darling, surely you understand my confusion." My aunt Gertrude was a florid woman holding court in one of the refurbished Ikea chairs, fanning herself slowly. The man sitting across from her was dressed in a black, finely tailored suit that downplayed the slight green tint to his complexion.

He leaned forward in a slight, mock bow. "Can't the Trade Minister call on the Garbage Queen? After all, you control quite a bit of the Earth artifact trade."

Auntie guffawed, slapping the plastic fan closed on her knee. "Now see, that's it right there. You came to see me, you with your pretty governmental position and influence, when you could very well have sent me a non-invitation invitation to come to your office. Which leads me to believe that what you're up to isn't strictly above board. That insults me, it does. All my scavengers are properly licensed and operate within the strict regulations laid down by your own office."

A smile flitted across the minister's face. "Which is why, I am sure, you're the only human wealthy or influential enough to own an apartment here in the Emerald City instead of out in one of the human slums along the desert's edge."

I finished arranging the tea on the table between them and retreated to my sewing corner, remaining close by in case Auntie needed anything else. The basket beside me was full of my failed attempts to learn embroidery, but Auntie insisted I keep trying, as it was a skill that an upper-class woman of Earth would have known. It didn't matter to her that it was a skill a woman hadn't needed to practice for three hundred years. I sighed, and picked up the lopsided rose I had been working on.

Elphred waited until I was settled, collecting his thoughts, then lowered his voice. "Of course, you heard about the large drop that happened out in Munchkinland yesterday?" He picked over the pastries until he found the one with the most icing. "Four F-5 tornadoes tore their way through Oklahoma, brought in about sixty refugees and a couple warehouses?" He paused to take a bite of the delicacy and hummed in appreciation. "You really do have the best fried rings. Where do you get them?"

Auntie snapped the fan open again. One of her frequent complaints about Oz was the lack of air conditioning. "Donuts, darling, they're called donuts. I make them myself, old family recipe. I can send a box of them with you. As for the drop, of course I heard—my crews brought in quite the haul from it."

"What your crews didn't get to see was a travel-pod that came through. A scientist by the name of Diggs, and his equipment. His pod was quite nice, too—a new line from Mitsubishi, it looks like. They finally figured out the pressurization problem." The minister's tongue flicked out to catch a stray bit of frosting at the corner of his mouth.

Auntie waited for him to continue, but when he simply popped the last piece of pastry in his mouth, she broke. "Well, are you gonna make me sit here all day, or are you going to tell me what your great, secret scientist is for?"

Elphred brushed his hands together to get rid of any lingering crumbs and picked up his cup of tea. The half smile was again hovering around his mouth. "He can stabilize a travel-storm."

I pricked my finger and swore, sticking it in my mouth before I could bleed all over the muslin. Auntie didn't notice or I would have received a lecture; instead, she was leaning across the table and her eyes had gone hard, the way they always did when she sensed a good bargain. The minister continued to carefully sip his tea.

"You're telling me that he figured out a way to stabilize the crossing? Is it safe?"

Elphred carefully laid his cup down before leaning back and folding his hands. "It is. Opens a doorway at ground level—not very big, mind you, but you could probably drive a pickup truck through it. No more thrashing about through tornados and praying you get here in one piece. No more picking up trash and trying to cobble it back together to sell to people desperate for a piece of their homeland."

Auntie's eyes narrowed as she tried to figure out Elphred's angle. "I'm sure he didn't bring it over solely for that reason."

"Oh, no, he had all sorts of humanitarian reasons—a safe, stable way for people to evacuate your 'global warming-ravaged earth.'" The minister actually used air quotes around the words of the human propaganda. I ducked my head to hide a smirk at how awkward the Earth mannerism looked on him. "There are apparently a lot of people willing to pay big bucks on your side of the veil to guarantee safe passage through the travel-storms. But we have enough refugees as it is, don't you think? Why would we open our lands to more if we could help it?"

"But a trade route from Earth, that...that could be very lucrative for all involved." Auntie leaned back, her fan picking up speed. "How do we know that you won't just use this as an opportunity to send us all back through the veil?"

The minister wrinkled his nose. "Princess Ozma...well, you've heard the stories. She's rather fond of you Earthers. If you started disappearing en masse, she would figure out that we have this device and would almost certainly use it to bring more of you over. Her...generosity knows no bounds. No, it is in everyone's interest if the only people who know about this are the people directly involved in a discreet inner circle."

"In that case, why come to me?" The two of them seemed to have forgotten that I was even in the room and I was glad for it. A way home—that's what they were talking about. I'd lived in Oz just about as long as I could remember and I would give anything to be able to go home again, even if Earth was being torn apart by humanity's greed; it was where I came from. My family had been ripped out of our home before anyone even realized that Oz was real and that we could get there by storm-jumping. Both my parents died in the crossing.

Elphred smiled broadly for the first time. "That should be obvious. You are the only trader of human goods, an expert in the supply and demand on this side of the veil. It would behoove me to partner with you to find out just what people on this side want and what the other side might need."

"This is an interesting proposition you've come to me with." I could tell from years of watching Auntie work that she was hooked, but she didn't want the green man to know it yet. Her eyes only glittered that way when she smelled money, and a lot of it. "How do I know I can trust you not to leave me and mine stranded on the other side of the veil?"

"Well, we'll just need to have a little oversight." He paused before he turned to me. "Forgive me, girl, but I forgot my manners entirely. I presume I have the pleasure of addressing Thea? Thea Gale?"

Auntie's head snapped around to stare at me as if she'd forgotten I'd existed. No one ever addressed me. I sat in the corner invisible unless somebody needed something. Then I was hardly better than a clockwork servant, sent to fetch and carry. None of her guests had known my name before. Auntie looked as though she might interrupt, but then gestured for me to answer.

"Yes, sir, my name's Thea." I put my sewing down and went to stand behind Auntie's shoulder. I didn't care for the way Elphred was studying me, and the bulk of my adoptive mother between me and him was a comfort.

"Well, Ms. Gertrude, I hear you've been training this one to be as beguiling as yourself across the negotiation tables. What if she came to the palace as my special guest and oversaw all the work? She can report back to you exactly what stage the testing is in and vanquish any fears you might have about our cheating you. Also, this way, no one gets suspicious about our spending too much time in each other's presence. That wouldn't be good for either of us."

Now, everything he said was true. I sat in on most deals Auntie made and knew a fair amount about the business, especially since I had a knack for numbers, though I was hardly the superior business woman Auntie was—nor was I anywhere near her level of crooked. I couldn't lie worth a damn. But I guess that made me ideal as a songbird.

"Seems fair enough to me. Thea, how's that sound to you?" Auntie's hand reached over to grasp mine, but her attention was focused on our guest. Her hand was clammy and shaking a bit, completely out of character for her. And when Auntie worries, I worry.

"I guess I can manage that. I mean, I won't be able to tell much on the science end of things, but I can tell you what I see. Plus, the palace is rather pretty, and I've never seen inside it." I smiled my fourth nicest smile at Elphred and squeezed Auntie's hand, trying to let her know I could tell she was worried, but I thought I could handle it.

"That's settled then. Thea, why don't you go get a few things packed while I talk to your aunt about the details and then we'll head over to your new quarters."

"What, immediately?" Auntie's hand tightened convulsively and Elphred smiled.

"I planned on starting the tests today and it'd be best to have a human on hand to verify that I am telling you the Oz-honest truth." Elphred hesitated just a hair too long for comfort. "Unless you have some objection?"

"I'll just be lonesome without her, she's the only family I have this side of the veil. However, if that's what you think is best—Thea, go get your stuff." She squeezed my hand one last time and let me go. "Just the basics." The trade minister called after me. "We'll get you a wardrobe at the palace more suitable to your surroundings."

I looked down at my threadbare Earth dress and smiled. Finally, I was going to get to wear something new. Bless Auntie's heart, but it would be nice not to have to let down another hem for a while. I pulled our biggest market basket out of the kitchen on my way to my little room and stood for a while, contemplating what I should bring with me. Everything in my room was of Earth origin, except for the walls themselves, and those were the rich green of the rest of the city. I'd mostly covered them with postcards of Earth that Auntie had given me from the scavenged drop sites. I didn't own much other than clothes and the minister had said I would not need those. Still, I pulled out a few undergarments and handkerchiefs.

The pile of gray fur on my pillow stretched and stepped carefully across my bed to twine around the basket. I scritched Mrow behind his ears before turning back to my dresser and pulling my journal from the underwear drawer. "I doubt you're allowed to come with me."

"You can't very well be expected to go to the palace without an escort, now, can you?" The cat wrapped his tail carefully around him as he sat in the basket, the very picture of innocence.

"It is true that Ozites have a different view of animals than we have on the other side, and, for a cat, you're remarkably well-behaved. But I'm headed over to be Auntie's eyes and ears, and I'm not entirely sure it's safe." I tucked the journal and my favorite pen into the basket beside Mrow and turned around my room, trying to decide if I was missing anything.

"All the more reason I should accompany you. I do not trust a single one of these Ozites as much as a mouse."

I smiled at his aloof tone. "You don't trust Earthers either."

He sniffed and settled farther into the basket. "Well, you aren't cats—what can you expect?"

6

I had to admit, his logic was unassailable.

The last thing I did before leaving my room was to put on my mother's locket. I didn't wear it all that much because I was afraid of losing it. But on this adventure, I felt like I could use the luck. I scooped up the basket, Mrow and all, and turned out my lamp before heading back to the living room. Auntie and the minister were talking, low and tense, and I hesitated before re-entering the room, wondering what was so whisper-inducing.

"We should have been informed immediately that a Gale had dropped."

"When I found her as a toddler, alone, I didn't know it was important. Later, I worried about what would happen to her. I do think of her as a daughter—you keep that in mind."

"Does she know who she is?"

"Of course not. Why burden her with it? She's still just a child, really; I've kept it away from her as best as possible. Besides, Gale isn't exactly an uncommon name. I never told her she was one of those Gales."

"Dorothy was a lot younger than her the first time she came over."

Mrow let out a chirrup and leaped from the basket to trot into the room. The conversation stopped abruptly and then Auntie called out, "Thea?"

I came around the corner and into the room, smiling as though I hadn't just overheard them talking about me and whatever danger being a Gale brought. It seemed entirely absurd that the government should take an interest in me, an orphaned Earther from Kansas. I hardly even remembered Earth, I'd dropped so long ago.

"Well, let me make up that list of things I think your first foray should bring back. I'll just be a minute." Auntie levered herself out of her chair and went into the kitchen. I was left facing the minister.

"Who is this handsome feline? Is he one of ours or one of yours?" Elphred held his hand out to Mrow, who took his time sniffing it over before presenting his ears for fluffing.

"That's Mrow, and he's an Earth cat. He's been with me since before I dropped. I'm not sure how he survived the ride, or even me

—7

for that matter. We were accidental refugees, my family and me." I wasn't sure why Mrow didn't speak up, but maybe he was taking that whole distrust thing rather more seriously than I thought.

The cat abandoned the green man's attentions and settled into my basket, purring loudly, eyes barely still open. The minister looked bemused. "I rather think he wants to come with you."

"So it would seem. Would it be alright? Auntie doesn't really get along with him anyway and since we don't know how long I'll be with you, could he come along, Minister?"

Mrow let out his namesake sound and reached up to dig one set of claws into the rim of the basket. Elphred's eyes narrowed. I played demure, eyes cast down and swished my skirt the way Auntie had taught me. "It would put me so much more at ease. I've never even been on the same street as the palace, let alone inside of it."

"Well, alright, if it gets us out the door faster, so be it. Just know, you'll be responsible for the beast. If he makes a mess or rips up the furniture or anything unsightly like that, you'll have to bring him back here." The green man stood, tugging his vest and jacket straight, then called into the kitchen. "If everything is settled, we'll be off. Ms. Gertrude? Everything to your satisfaction?"

My aunt came scurrying back in and handed me a list. "Right as rain. Now let me say my goodbyes and she'll meet you down at your carriage."

The Minister tugged at a cuff. "I can wait."

I could tell that wasn't what Auntie wanted, but she couldn't kick him out, not if she wanted to keep the sweet deal she was going to be getting. I wished I could interrogate her, but it would have to wait. So we kept our goodbyes brief, with Auntie giving me a stern reminder to behave myself like a young lady and to report everything back to her regularly and to not forget anything on her rather lengthy list. Her hands shook on my shoulders and I could feel how cold they were through the thin material of my dress. But I took them and kissed them, then her cheek, and told her I'd be just fine. After all, I had Mrow with me, and if we could survive a travel-storm, we could survive anything.

2

I wasn't lying when I said I had never seen the inside of the palace. As such, I was suitably impressed when Minister Elphred's carriage wove its way up the main boulevard and into the roundabout at the main entrance. The sprawling towers meandered over almost two acres of the city, with no real pattern or plan that I could see. It was all true emerald green, some portions even looking like they were carved from their namesake rock.

I had heard legends about how the city was originally white and everyone just wore green glasses. When they tried to do away with the glasses, no one could see properly for the shining of it all, so the witches had gotten together and figured out a way to make everything green for real. To be honest, I was rather sick of the color and did everything I could at home to cover it up.

A footman opened my door and I stepped out with my basket, craning my neck to look up to the top of the grand entranceway. Only a small door was open for us, cut into the larger doors, and I wondered just how heavy the main doors were to open.

"After you, Miss Thea." Elphred gestured for me to precede him and I did, happily forgetting the danger Auntie had implied was lurking and letting myself dive into the grandeur and opulence before me. The vestibule was as large as our whole apartment complex, with staircases and hallways winding away into the distance. The whole spectacle was topped off by green crystal chandeliers lit even this early in the day.

"I'm not 'miss' anything, Minister, I'm just plain Thea." I stepped aside to let him in after me without having to give up my perspective of the main hall. Mrow was purring again, hard enough to make his basket rock.

"As you wish. We'll be staying in the west wing and I've arranged for a suite just next to mine, with the good doctor across the hall. We'll be able to work together and be uninterrupted for the time being." He strode down the hall and I had to scramble to catch up, my black flats sliding on the polished stone.

"Do you think I'll see Ozma while I'm here?" I'd always heard such wonderful stories about the fairy princess, and I rather hoped he'd say yes.

"I'm afraid not. Ozma doesn't live here full time anymore—she prefers one of the outlying palaces, away from the bustle of the government she created. This building is almost entirely given over to governmental function and the apartments for the ministers and guests who need to be...impressed upon."

"Oh." After a moment's hesitation, I added, "I guess that makes our job a little easier, doesn't it?"

A small smile played at the corner of Elphred's mouth as he strode along. "That it does. Here is your room. You'll find the closet stocked with more appropriate clothing, and everything should be in your size. A maid will be along shortly—let her know if things don't fit properly. I shall expect you for dinner in a half hour in my chambers, where I will introduce you to the doctor and then we can get to work. Until then." He clicked his heels together and gave an abbreviated bow, then left me standing in my open doorway.

"Well. I guess it's a good thing I didn't have any urgent questions," I told Mrow, a bit annoyed.

"I rather think he'd have avoided answering any of the interesting ones anyway." He leapt out of the basket, nearly causing me to drop

11

it, and sauntered into the room. "At least our quarters are bigger than that rat hole you call an apartment."

I had to agree with the cat. Our entire apartment—all three bedrooms, kitchen, and living room—could have fit in the sitting room of my new suite. I dropped my basket on a divan and wandered through one of the doorways to find myself in a spa-like bathroom that included a green glass air-jet tub. I was definitely going to have to try that out later. My current goal was to find the bedroom and wardrobe that the Minister had promised.

The next door I tried led to the bedroom, complete with an enormous four-poster feather bed. I sighed, thinking I was going to have to sleep on the couches since down and I did not particularly get along, but made my way to the standing wardrobe. I threw open the doors to find rack after rack of high Ozite fashion. There were gorgeous silks and satins in a dizzying array of greens and I couldn't wait to try some of it on. I chose a delicate seafoam number and hurriedly stripped out of my worn gingham.

After five minutes, Mrow was rolling on the floor laughing and I had to admit defeat. I'd never had the opportunity to wear Ozite fashion since Auntie didn't allow it, saying we needed to stay proud of our Earth heritage, and the array of ties and fobs and clips and buttons on this dress had soundly outsmarted me.

"Oh dear, that's entirely wrong."

I scrambled to cover myself but relaxed at the site of a clockwork maid in the doorway. She was a newer model, rather delicately featured, and she moved with a stuttering grace, belying her clockwork nature.

I smiled, a bit embarrassed, and tried to disentangle myself from the mess I'd created. "Sorry, it's my first time with this kind of clothing and I just...it doesn't make sense."

"Here, let me." She came over and had me extricated in a few moments. She hesitated at the knife sheathed on my thigh, but said nothing. With another few swift movements she had me properly clothed and tied up. "My name is Clack-tick. I'll be your maid while you're here."

Her voice was bland and didn't betray the usual anger I heard when I talked with other Ozites in the marketplace. "It doesn't bother you that you were assigned to an Earther?"

"To be honest, I volunteered. I was curious. I'm only a few months old and I've never seen an Earther." She swept around the room, gathering my old Earth dress and holding it up to study its shape, before draping it over her arm. "I'll take this to be cleaned." The maid hesitated before blurting, "Do you mind...that is, were you an intentional?"

I smiled and shook my head. "Me? No, I've been here since I was small. My family was picked up in the first couple years of severe global warming by one of the travel-storms and dropped here before we knew it wasn't suicide to go running into tornadoes. At least, not guaranteed suicide. All my family still died. I was raised by Ms. Gertrude."

Clack-tick's eyes lit up a startling shade of orange. "The Garbage Queen."

"Well, yes. Do you know her?"

"Not personally, but her company finds some of the most delicious oils and lubricants. You Earthers sure know how to take care of a machine."

I was really starting to like Clack-tick. "Well, I'll see if Auntie has anything lying about the next time I see her."

"Perhaps she has some WD-40? That stuff is simply...divine. I've only ever had a drop or two." Her eyes brightened and she gave a happy little jangle.

"I think we have some. I'll be sure to bring it." I spun, trying to see all of myself in the full-length mirror. "What do you think? Can I pass as an Ozite in this dress?" The wraparound dress draped a little too well, and I wondered how long the Minister had been planning to request my presence.

"Just so. No one will be able to tell the difference until you talk."

I shot her a wry smile before going back to playing with the silk. "Thanks for that."

"Oh! No, I only meant that you have a beautiful Earther accent...I wouldn't change it for anything."

"Well, thanks. I guess I'll go see if the Minister is ready for dinner, even though I'm a bit early. I'd rather get started on this project."

"Yes, of course. Can I get anything else for you?"

Mrow started up a pathetic pantomime on the floor, letting out piteous meows, to indicate that he was dying of starvation. "If you have a plate of tuna for my cat, it would not go amiss. He's a rascal, though. Don't let him con you into anything richer; he's supposed to be losing weight."

"Of course! The mighty animal needs to keep up his strength." Clack-tick leaned down to tickle Mrow's stomach and he promptly swiped at her metal arm, creating a screech that set my teeth on edge. "How adorable and fierce!"

"If you say so. Mrow, behave yourself: I'll see you in a bit."

I made my way back to the hall and then down to the door marked with Elphred's name and title. I knocked briefly and opened the door to find the green man hastily setting down a large snowglobe. "Oh, forgive me, I'm early."

"No, please, come in. The food should be brought up shortly and our scientist will be joining us at any moment." He gestured toward a table set up in the middle of the room.

I made my way over and he held out a chair for me. I was reluctant to put my back to him, but it would have been rude to decline, so I sat, jarred a little as he pushed the chair in faster than was strictly necessary.

There was a moment of silence and I scrambled for a topic of conversation. "That was a pretty snowglobe you were holding when I came in. I wasn't aware they made them on this side of the Veil...or is it Earth-made?"

"This?" Elphred picked it back up, but made no motion to let me see it better. He swirled it around, smiling faintly. "No, no, it was made over here. A long time ago, in fact. It was my Grandmother's; before she passed away, she gave it to me. It's not much more than a bauble, but it's the only thing I have left of her."

I kicked myself mentally. Of course I'd fixate on the one thing in the room that created an awkward conversation. "I'm sorry, I didn't mean to bring up any painful memories."

"Oh, they are not so much painful anymore as nostalgic. I have some beautiful memories of Grandmother from when I was very young." There was a knock at the door and Elphred put down the snowglobe and strode over to answer it.

"Dr. Diggs, how good of you to join us! Please, come in." A rather unimpressive young man in a worn leather jacket entered, his hair in disarray. He reached out and grabbed the older man's hand, shaking vigorously.

"Minister, thank you again for your hospitality. I wasn't sure what kind of facilities I'd have to work with or whether I'd just be in an open field and, let me tell you, this palace is far beyond what I could have hoped for."

"Yes, yes, we're glad we could be of some help to you in your efforts. I know it's important to you to get the travel-storm phenomena sorted out as soon as possible." Elphred guided Dr. Diggs into the room and shut the door. "However, this evening, I'd like to introduce you to an influential young woman in our city, Miss Thea Gale." I stood, offering my hand to the doctor, surprised at how young he was.

"A pleasure to meet you, a real pleasure." He smiled as we shook hands, though he seemed distracted by something I couldn't see.

"And you, Doctor. I hear you have a way that might actually let me see my home dimension and let me live to talk about it." I gently disengaged my hand and sat again.

The two men joined me at the table. "Well, yes, I suppose I do, though the purpose is more for bringing people over here rather than sending people back. Our world is falling to pieces and trying to take the human race with it. It is imperative that we find someplace to salvage what we can. Isn't that right, Minister?"

"Please, Elphred will do. We're all friends here. And, yes, our goal is to stabilize a connection with your world." I noticed he didn't say what for, and I wasn't going to speak up. I was this close to actually getting to see my world and didn't want to ruin it by spoiling Elphred's plans, even if I personally thought they were despicable.

Maybe I would be able to convince him to let through some refugees later along with his trade shipments. He probably would, if they were willing to pay enough.

I twiddled with my napkin while I waited for our food to arrive. "Dr. Diggs, how was it you managed to figure it out? Stabilizing a travel-storm, I mean. It's not like you've had a lot of time to study this sort of thing, since it's a fairly new phenomena."

Elphred laughed. "Oh, Diggs here isn't a stranger to our world, are you?"

"No, I'm not. Well, not entirely, I should say, since this is my first trip over. My great-grandfather wrote down some incredible stories about this other world, Oz, that he'd managed to get to by flying through a storm. Most of the family thought he was just nuts, but I couldn't let it go. I have dual degrees in meteorology and physics, specifically multiple dimension theory. It wasn't until those storm hunters were caught in a travel-storm and actually managed to transmit data from this side that my work was taken seriously. Let me tell you, the funding came pouring in."

A bell chime interrupted his explanation, and three Munchkins came in with heavily laden trays. They moved in synchronicity, placing the trays in front of us, removing the lids, and bowing before retreating through the same door they had entered from. They left behind beds of lettuce with dollops of three-bean salad, egg salad, tuna salad, chicken salad, pasta salad, potato salad, and a few other sticky, creamy masses I couldn't identify.

"I heard that on warm evenings like this, Earthers occasionally just eat a salad, but I wasn't sure what kind of salads you two would prefer, so I had them give each of you a variety. Please, dig in." Elphred spread his napkin in his lap and started to pick at the pasta salad on his plate.

"Thank you, egg salad is my favorite." Dr. Diggs picked up his fork and dug in with gusto while I sighed and silently wished for a steak. I settled for tuna salad instead and ate quietly while the two men talked science that went straight over my head. We finished in short order and Elphred suggested a walk over to the doctor's quarters to see his equipment, now that it was all set up and calibrated.

"The only part I don't quite understand is the formation of an actual travel-storm as compared to a basic storm on Earth," the doctor said. "We know that not all of the major storms split the veil between our worlds, but we have yet to figure out what the difference is. We know travel-storms are stronger and much deadlier, hence all the advancements we're making in travel-pods. All my machine can do is latch on to a tear when it forms and stabilize it until it closes. The units on either side of the veil anchor it at ground level in a single spot for safer passage. Our machines here will be able to link with the ones on Earth during the next travel-storm and we'll be able to pass things through. Really, I can't tell you how excited I am to finally be testing this."

"As am I, doctor. Truly." We had entered the lab at this point, and I wondered at Elphred's patience with the Earther scientist. He just went on and on and it was hard to get a word in edgewise. I wanted to get to the hole-making so I could see Earth again. The room had an arch big enough for a large vehicle to pass through, with a bank of large machines wired to it. Surprisingly, they were on.

I interrupted the doctor as he was explaining to Elphred the physics of latching on to a travel-storm. "How are your machines working? There isn't electricity over here, and their electromagic doesn't work over there, so you can't design a machine around it."

The doctor scowled at my interruption, but cleared his throat and leaned over me, as if I were a small child. "Well, I had designed a generator to run on steam power, but Minister Elphred here had a better idea."

Elphred held up his hand and played with a spark that he sent dancing through his fingers. "I simply juiced up his capacitors myself. Old family trick."

The spark crackled and evaporated and the green man rubbed his hands together briskly, ignoring me once more. "Are we ready to turn this on and link up with its brother machine?"

"Well, we'll need to wait for a travel-storm, since we can't create the link without one, but—" The doctor was interrupted by a siren and whirling red light going off on top of the machine. "What providence! We have one now."

"Yes, what luck." Elphred tucked his hands carefully into his pockets and stepped back from the machines, smiling. Dr. Diggs didn't notice, as all of his attention was now focused on his machines and computers, punching in commands and tweaking dials. I carefully avoided looking at Elphred as he retreated behind me to a divan at the back of the room; I didn't want him to notice me noticing that he wasn't surprised in the slightest by the travel-storm's arrival.

There was a fierce electric crackle filling the air and the arch began to glow and pulse with miniature lightning. I decided the back of the room with a shifty Elphred was probably safer than the new machines, even with my misgivings, and retreated to his side. "Are you sure this won't just blow up? I mean, has he even had the opportunity to turn it on since he got over here?"

"No, not as such, but I have faith." I could smell the ozone of gathered power surrounding him and I edged away a bit.

"Which is why you're gathering a force field around you, I'm sure." His lips quirked in a faint smile. "While I have faith, it doesn't hurt to hedge your bets." He made a small gesture and the bubble of power around him expanded to include me as well. I shivered as the wave of it passed through me, not liking the cold sensation, and liking even less that he hadn't asked.

"I didn't realize you were a witch. I'm afraid I've never met one before."

"What makes you think I'm not a fairy?" Elphred was watching the doctor with great concentration.

"Well, the stories say they all left ages ago…all except Ozma, that is."

The green man snorted. "Stories are often wrong. For example, Ozma is hardly the fairy princess they sing about."

"What is she then?"

A blinding white flash of light and a clap of thunder reverberated through the room, and when I could see again, Dr. Diggs was leaning through the archway into a white sterile laboratory, conversing with two young Earther adults, one a tall gangly man, the other a much stouter woman. Elphred was standing at his machines, studying the settings and readouts, ignoring everything else around him. I made my way over to the archway, still reeling a bit from the blast of the connection.

"The flowmeter?"

"Stable."

"How are the energy readouts on the flux capacitor?"

"I told you, Jason, we're not naming it that. It's the Diggs Stabilizer."

"Fine. How are the energy readouts on the Diggs Stabilizer?"

"Normal. Perfectly normal! It worked!" The three scientists shook hands across the threshold as I came up behind Diggs.

"Could...I mean, if you're through making sure it's safe, might I go over? Just for a minute?"

Diggs turned and smiled. "Of course, dear girl, of course. Make it quick; we don't know how long the connection will last."

I took a deep breath, closed my eyes, and stepped through the thin wavering light between me and Earth. The air instantly felt different; dry and too thin, compared to the atmosphere of Oz. I peered around the laboratory before going over to a window to look out at Earth. "Where are we? I don't see any storm."

"Canada, Ontario. Its relatively tornado-free and the extreme temperatures don't get as bad up here during the summer. The storm is actually centered over..." Jason consulted a readout. "Oklahoma right now. It's a doozy too. Good thing all that land is just corporate farm now." Jason came up to stand behind me. "Beautiful, isn't it?"

It wasn't. It was dull and bleak. There were hardly any trees, and a strong wind was whipping up dust clouds that occasionally obscured the window. The colors lacked any sort of vibrancy, the life they had in Oz. My skin itched with the emptiness of the air and I shivered. "I think I'll go back now. Just, you know, so I don't get stranded."

I retreated back through the arch and settled unsteadily into a chair by the door. Earth had felt so wrong. I had felt like I couldn't breathe—it all just seemed so dead compared to here. Even the fabric of the chair under me felt like it could come to life at any moment. Which, in reality, it could. I shuddered as the last of the itchy feeling left my skin, soothed by the wash and flow of the power of Oz.

"...no, once we lose the storm, the connection will snap. We're not sure what would happen to anything in the field when that happens. I wouldn't recommend connecting to every storm, either. This field generator puts a great deal of stress on the veil and I can't guarantee we won't start damaging it. Who knows what kind of effect that would have." Dr. Diggs was recording some numbers off of one of the screens and Elphred was peering through the arch when it gave an audible pop and the other laboratory vanished. Elphred jerked his head back and rubbed his nose at the backwash of power.

"Fascinating. Tell me more about the stress on the veil. Does it depend on the amount of matter going back and forth?"

"Not so far as I can tell. It seems the greater stress is on our side— while you get dumps of physical objects and people, the storms are ripping into our reality with a foreign energy that our physics just don't know how to respond to properly. It breaks apart the basic laws of our reality in a localized area for a short period of time."

They started to wax technical again and I tuned them out. I was shaking from my encounter with my home world and just wanted to curl up under a blanket until I figured out whether I was disappointed. This morning I still thought I'd never be able to see Earth again and now...I don't think I wanted to go through the veil again. But I was an Earther! All I should want is to go back, to see it once more, to run across the hay fields on my family's farm.

I stood abruptly, causing the two men to pause in their conversation. "I'm feeling a bit shaky. Today has been rather overstimulating, I'm afraid. Do please excuse me, gentlemen." They acknowledged me with a nod and a wave before going back to the nitty-gritty bits of their machine.

I was so preoccupied by trying to figure out how to feel about having just been on Earth again that I accidentally entered Elphred's room instead of mine. I stopped as soon as I noticed the dinner table, and had turned to leave when my eye was caught by the snowglobe. I had always loved snowglobes, and decided that a look couldn't hurt. It was rather large, so I didn't pick it up, but I peered in, marveling at how the glitter and sand inside of it was moving independently of any motion on my part. It was swirling hard enough to mostly obscure the interior, but calmed as I watched, so that I could see that it was empty of any figures or props. Instead, a small map of Oklahoma was under its clear base.

"Hsst...Thea!" Mrow was in a doorway that I could only assume led back to Elphred's bedroom.

"How'd you get in here?"

"Secret panel, but I can hear them coming from down the hall, so you better follow me, fast." I hurried after him and ducked into the wardrobe in the bedroom, carefully closing the false panel behind me.

"Why in Oz is there a false panel between our rooms, and how did you open it?" I straightened the clothes in my closet, then had the idea of taking the chair from the vanity and wedging it against the false back. I didn't want Elphred to be able to use that panel later.

"I would wager it's so he can keep an eye on you, but that's just paranoid ol' me." Mrow sat and began to vigorously wash his hind leg.

"Like that's not creepy. Nor the fact that he was playing with this great big snowglobe that had a map of Oklahoma under it and then the travel-storm that hit this evening was tearing apart the same state." I struggled at the fasteners on the dress; they were just out of reach.

"Need some help?" Mrow unsheathed his claws and began to carefully clean them as well.

I rolled my eyes and managed to get the dress off over my head. "Seriously, do you think that might be what causes the travel-storms? That ball?"

"What, and he's aiming them at Oklahoma? There's not much there."

"Just farms apparently." I paused as I pulled a much simpler green shift over my head. "Which brings over all the produce it rips out the ground, which a savvy Minister of Trade might take advantage of."

"But no one knows how or where the travel-storms form. What makes you think this globe might do it?"

"One, he's a witch."

"I could have told you that. He reeks of magic."

I made a face at the cat and flounced on the bed. "Two, he was playing with the globe before dinner. After dinner, there was conveniently a travel-storm, and then when I accidentally wandered into his room—"

"Sure, accidentally." I threw a pillow at my cat. He avoided it, then joined me on the bed.

"Accidentally. It was still swirling and then it finally settled down and I could see the map of Oklahoma." I started scratching Mrow in his favorite spot, just under his chin, and he started purring.

He paused just long enough to concede that I might have a point, then returned to blissfully accepting my attention.

"The question becomes, is any of that important?"

Mrow pulled away to roll over onto his back. "How about you just give me a note to drag across town and let Gertrude decide for herself?"

"I think I will do just that." I spent the next half hour composing a note to Auntie telling her everything that had happened since I had arrived, cutting out the touristy bits near the beginning and the uncomfortable ones Earth-side, then folded it up and tucked it under Mrow's basket for him to take to Auntie in the morning. I hoped she would have some idea of how to handle this charged situation, or else I'd be forced to take drastic, and probably irresponsible, action.

# 3

I woke once during the night and thought I heard a thumping coming from my wardrobe, but it stopped before I could properly identify it. I smiled at the thought of the chair in the way of the secret panel and then fell back asleep.

By the time I woke properly the next morning, Mrow had slipped out with the note for Auntie. I wished him a speedy journey through the city and a quick return; I felt strangely alone without his solid bulk at the end of my bed.

A brief knock at the door announced Clack-tick's presence before she whirred in and began opening my blinds. "It is a lovely day out there, Miss Thea. A whole ton of corn fell in Munchkinland last night. They say it did a bit of property damage, but at least they weren't dropping houses on top of anyone this time!"

I laughed with her, uneasy at the reminder that I might have discovered where those storms were coming from. Stumbling out of bed, I made my way through my morning ablutions before letting Clack-tick rope me into another green dress, this one an elegant ensemble in a rich forest green. It took a couple tries to get all of the long strips of fabric tied properly, but they gave a strangely fluid motion to the finished product. I found myself swaying in front of the mirror to watch all the different panels of the dress catch the air and move in different directions.

"I'll never get used to these."

Clack-tick was already tidying my bed. "Of course you will, but breakfast is cooling in your sitting room. Do you need anything else this morning?"

"Nope, I should be just fine." I tore myself away from the mirror and had started towards the sitting room when Clack-tick spoke up again.

"I don't mean to pry, but is Mrow about this morning? I brought him a saucer of cream and a breakfast of mackerel."

"You are spoiling him." I couldn't help but smile at the thought of how delighted the furry nuisance would be when he got back from his errand. "He went out to do his business earlier, but I'm sure he'll return soon. I take it you got along with him yesterday?"

"Oh, yes, he's a charming fellow, with quite a wicked sense of humor." She fluffed the pillows and followed me into the main room.

"I'm surprised he spoke to you. He tends to keep quiet in front of strangers." I sat at the table and pushed out another chair for Clack-tick to sit with me.

"I'm sure it was just to try and convince me to bring him cream last night, but we talked about all sorts of things. He was rather interested in some of the older stories, from before Ozma came to power. We're not really supposed to gossip about these things, but did you know that Minister Elphred is descended from the great Witch of the West herself? She was his grandmother. Rumor has it that the Earther who was impersonating the Wizard impregnated her, then sent another Earther, Dorothy Gale, to kill her. He never let the prejudice against his family stop him, though."

At the name Gale, things started to come together for me. "Gale, you say? She wouldn't have happened to be a Kansas resident, would she?"

Clack-tick picked at a nick in the breakfast tray and nibbled on a scrap of silver. "You know, now that you mention it, I think she was. The stories of the havoc she created are hilarious—you should see some of the plays we have about it."

"I'll look into that, thanks. They sound fascinating." I picked at the food on my plate, but any semblance of appetite I had was gone. "Clack-tick, do you know when Elphred is expecting me this morning?"

"He said to tell you that he'll be in the laboratory when you're ready."

"Thanks. You know, I'm not all that hungry. I think I'll just take my tea over there, if you don't mind." I picked up the mug, happy to have it to warm my fingers; they were freezing as my mind raced over all the things I had learned in the last day. One, I'm descended from the most famous character in Oz history, barring Ozma herself. Two, I was dealing with the descendent of the woman my ancestor was supposed to have murdered. I wasn't sure how much more complicated things could get, at this point.

"Certainly. Should I leave the tray here or...?"

"Go ahead and leave it for now, thank you. I may change my mind later." We walked out into the corridor together and exchanged pleasantries before parting ways. It was as if the two men hadn't even left the night before; in fact, they were still wearing the same clothes and were just as deeply immersed in technical discussions as they had been when I left them. The only difference in the room was the addition of several trays of food—and Elphred's snowglobe on the corner of a desk in the center of the room. That must have been what he had gone to get from his room while I was snooping. I wondered if he'd told Dr. Diggs what it did or if he had made some other excuse to bring it over.

I put my mug down on one of the clear spots of the table and tried to make sense of what the two men were saying, but it was incomprehensible numbers and jargon. I walked over to the arch and ran my hand over the edge of the metal.

"Be careful with that! We have it set so when the next storm hits, it'll automatically activate." Dr. Diggs hurried over to me and shepherded me away from his equipment.

I looked at the swirling water in the snowglobe on the table, watching it a moment as it started picking up speed, then turned to Elphred. The thought of him deliberately sending these deadly storms to my home world made me feel sick. "We don't have much longer to wait, do we? I think we're just about to get a storm."

The klaxon went off and the light began to swirl and with the same flash-bang as the night before, the connection was made with the Earth-based laboratory.

Dr. Diggs was frantically running from machine to machine. "Two in 24 hours! This is almost unheard of. How did you guess? We've never been able to predict them."

"I didn't guess. Minister Elphred generated it, didn't you?" I reached for the snowglobe, but the green man stepped between me and the focus of my attention, sliding it back from the edge of the table.

"Now, what would lead you to believe that? The storms are natural phenomena, occurring in the rift between our worlds."

I laughed. "Nothing about this world is natural, it's all magical. The storms are no different. That snowglobe—you got it from your grandmother, the Wicked Witch of the West, a woman known for her magical skill. Who's to say she didn't figure out a way to rip through the veil? It's sad that she didn't realize she'd bring her own demise through the veil."

The green man's eyes flashed, actually sparking in his anger. "That Earther bitch didn't kill my grandmother, only scarred her for life. She was hideous afterwards, and my mother barely lived long enough to birth me and then left me there in that castle, with nothing but a bitter cripple and all the time in the world to learn her magic." Elphred collected himself and smoothed his jacket compulsively. Sparks jumped back and forth from the wool material to his fingers.

"What's the real reason you are so eager to make this work? I mean, really?" I walked over to the machines and slapped one on the side. I was shaking, but if I backed down now, I'd probably just be dead before I could tell anyone else what I'd figured out. If my grandmother, or whatever, had managed to best his grandmother, the odds were in my favor, right? "I bet it's not for trade or immigration, or anything remotely beneficial for either Earth or Oz."

Elphred narrowed his eyes, and then came to some sort of decision. "You're entirely right. And now I'm going to have to speed up the timetable because you're just as nosy as that little Kansas whore." The minister made his way over to Dr. Diggs. "Your services are no longer needed, cousin."

"Cousin? I, what—" was all the man managed before Elphred downed him with a rather large electrical pulse. I hoped it wasn't strong enough to kill the scientist, and decided to keep touching the machine in case Elphred tried to do the same to me. The electrical current would carry through me and fry his equipment.

Instead, he stalked over to the snowglobe and gave it an especially vicious swirl. "That should keep the storm going until I can get the feedback loop started."

"Feedback loop?" That didn't sound good, not in the slightest. I peered around the edge of the machine to see what he was doing with the dials.

"Feedback, to set up a recycling of power through the storm with these nifty machines here. It will keep the rift open and growing between our worlds until the instability it introduces to your Earth is so great that it rips the planet to pieces. You Earthers are a plague. Every time you make it over here, you destroy something else. Your refugees take and take without any thought as to how they can give back. I can think of no more fitting audience to Earth's destruction than the descendants of that blithering idiot wizard and the gingham-wearing bitch who ruined more lives than she ever knew." Elphred had made his way over to the capacitors and grabbed them, crackling with energy that he fed into the machines, more and more until the sheath of power that swirled around him paled and then finally disappeared.

I wasn't sure if he had drained himself into the machine or just reduced his power levels, but I hoped that he'd let it all go—otherwise, what I was going to do next was really stupid.

Slowly taking my hand off the side of the machine, I started inching towards the snowglobe. If I could just grab it and break it, or remove the map, or something, that should stop the travel-storm. Right? I told myself yes again. I wasn't sure what else to try, but seeing as it controlled the storms, it seemed fairly logical. I could have tried messing with the machines, but that might just make things worse.

"Stop!" I froze in place, halfway between the snowglobe and the machines, not sure which way I should leap, but I was too slow. Elphred grabbed my wrist, spinning me away from the globe, and I could feel my hair start to stand on end. Apparently he wasn't so drained after all, but I wasn't dead yet, so that was something.

"You are going to stand here and watch." He yanked me in front of the arch, hard enough to make me yelp. Off-balance, I fell to the floor beside him, my arm still in his grip.

On the other side of the portal, you could already see the strain of the warring physics from either side of the veil. Sinkholes were opening in the floor of the lab and outside the window, storms swirled against each other. A hum started to fill the room, ugly and sour, making my teeth and stomach ache.

I could feel the tears on my face, and whether they were for my home world or just from the pain in my arm, I wasn't sure. "You don't need to do this! You have me—isn't it just my family you're so mad at? Mine and Dr. Diggs? Why can't you just punish us and leave our world alone?"

"You're a plague, that's why. Have you seen the shape your world is in? Constant war and disease and famine. You Earthers need to be wiped out once and for all to keep you from finding your way across the border ever again."

My attention was drawn away from the arch by a flicker of gray at the corner of my eye and I looked away just in time to see Mrow's tail disappear behind a table. I almost laughed with relief, but carefully kept the grimace on my face, which was not hard with the torque being applied to my shoulder.

Elphred was grinning, wide and hard, fixated on the destruction on the other side of the arch. "Almost—it's almost reached a self-sustaining threshold."

"But it's all for nothing without the magic your grandmother left you, right? Your globe? Won't that be useless once you destroy Earth since it controls the travel-storms? It might as well just be a broken pile of glass at that point."

"That doesn't matter. I'll have rid the worlds of you and that will be worth more than all the magical trinkets in my world." He turned to gesture at the globe and blanched, seeing Mrow casually rubbing up against said trinket. "No!" He tried to lunge for my cat, but I caught him around the knees and brought him down while Mrow worked the globe closer to the edge of the table.

It hurt, trying to pin the larger man with a shoulder on fire, but Auntie hadn't wanted any of her people to be helpless against the ravages of other scavengers, and she had taught me well. I pinched and pried at the delicate places, not so different on a witch's body than an Earther's, and Elphred screamed, half in rage, half in pain. He came back at me, trying to dislodge my arms from his body and I flipped over, using his momentum to toss him back towards the arch while I went for my knife.

He was lying half across the threshold when the sound of shattering glass filled a suddenly silent room. Mrow let out a perfectly innocent "Whoops!" before the room was filled with tearing winds and a torrential downpour. I threw myself under the nearest table and tried to protect myself from the flying debris. The storm faded quickly, and it took me a moment to realize that the pounding I was hearing was at the door to the laboratory rather than from the storm. I didn't know how the door had gotten locked, but it was and I hurried over to open it, shaking from the chill of the sudden downpour. Armed guards started to run in, and then slowed as they took in the wreck of the room, tapestries torn from the walls and furniture in broken, sodden pieces. Mrow sat on a table in the middle of it all, muttering to himself and desperately trying to clean his fur. Dr. Diggs still hadn't moved and was facedown in a puddle, so I hurried to his side as the guards stood stupidly around the room. I struggled to turn him over and then tried to find a pulse.

"Are you all going to stand their staring, or will one of you call a doctor?" I sighed in relief when Dr. Diggs started to cough and brought up a lungful of water. I propped him upright and turned to find the guards staring at the arch. "What?"

I came back around the tables and finally saw what they were staring at. "Well I guess that answers the question of what happens when you collapse the tear with something in it." Elphred's legs and the bottom half of his torso pointed towards the arch, but beyond the arch, there was nothing. "Good riddance," I muttered to myself. I started to shake in earnest and sat down hard on the one couch that had remained upright. A guard came over and unbuttoned his coat and draped it silently over my shoulders. The captain of the squad finally came to his senses and started snapping orders before coming over and sitting beside me on the divan.

"I know you've just been through a terrible shock, miss, but we need to know what happened here."

I sniffed and wiped at my face, trying to remove some of the water and grit, while giving myself a little extra time to think. I knew now that my family had a strong history with this place, and a not altogether happy one. I didn't know who that would matter to, or who I might have to answer to for what had just happened, so I gave an extra hard shudder and sobbed out, "The machines, they just…oh, it was horrible."

I dropped my head to his shoulder and started to cry. The tears weren't even faked; I hurt something fierce, my adrenaline was rapidly fading, and I was starting to freeze. He gestured for a guard to come and take me from the room, giving the man whispered instructions before letting me leave.

I was taken to my quarters where Clack-tick was anxiously waiting for me. She informed me that news traveled fast and asked whether I was hurt. I mumbled no. She shooed me into the bedroom, leaving the guard at my front door, and started to help me out of the soaked silks. I cried out when she tried to take the dress off my injured shoulder and she tsked and said yes, I did indeed need a doctor, but after a hot bath. I wasn't going to argue.

I hadn't been submerged in the blissfully hot water long when a gentle pat at the door preceded Mrow into the room. He was already looking quite fluffy and informed me that Clack-tick had a hair-dryer of sorts built into her arm.

"So, what are you going to say?" He leaped onto the thick tile edge of the tub and sat, tail curled around his feet to ensure it didn't accidentally get any wetter.

I sighed, and slipped farther into the tub. "I don't know. The truth seems awfully dangerous right now."

"Mmm." He narrowed his eyes in thought and sat silent for a moment. "May I make a suggestion?"

"I couldn't stop you if I wanted to."

"Very true. At any rate, this was a tragic accident. Minister Elphred had gathered together three people from families that were once enemies in an effort at finding some peace, through working on a machine to stabilize and neutralize the danger of crossing between our worlds, but due to an unforeseen mechanical malfunction, he tragically died."

I thought about it for a moment, swirling the water back and forth. "You think that's the best direction to go with it?"

"It does two things. One, it absolves you of any responsibility. You could even play up his heroic role in all of it. Two, it lets the world know who you are while at the same time negating the danger from any who may have been loyal to Elphred. Well, at least some of the danger. The truth about your lineage was bound to come out sooner or later anyway, but in this fashion you at least get to control its impact."

I stared at my cat, astounded at his deviousness. "You know, with a mind like yours, Auntie should have been taking business advice from you for years."

"What makes you think she hasn't been?" Mrow leaped down from the tub and started to make his way out of the bathroom when I had a thought.

"What about the doctor?"

Mrow snorted. "His brains got so fried, I doubt he'll even remember his own name in the morning."

# 4

A week later, Dr. Diggs, Mrow, and I stood outside the receiving hall at the palace. Diggs listed a bit to one side and had a tendency to drool, but other than that seemed to have come out of the ordeal without major injury. Mrow had been right that he remembered nothing from the day of the "accident." My arm was in a sling, but the shoulder was healing quickly, and no one had even commented on the hand-shaped electrical burn on my forearm. I'd had a story ready about how Elphred had yanked me out of harm's way when the machines began to malfunction, and I was disappointed I hadn't gotten to use it. But Mrow had repeated constantly over the last week to keep the lie simple; it was easier to remember that way.

We were waiting for our summons in to see Ozma and I was more than a little nervous. It was the first time I was going to meet the fairy ruler, and I wasn't sure what to expect. This was a formal ceremony to receive honors, posthumously in Elphred's case, and I felt like a total cheat.

The trumpets blew and I had no more time for rumination. I stood straight in the kelly-green ballgown I'd been shoehorned into and strode into the hall with Mrow and Dr. Diggs. At the end of the much-too-long hall, we stopped in front of Her Highness and I curtsied while Mrow blinked and Diggs tried to bow. He wobbled a bit.

The murmur of the crowded hall was making me even more nervous. I wasn't sure how many people in the hall were here to gawk at a descendant of Dorothy, and how many were here because they had known that Elphred would never have willingly made peace with me.

Ozma held up her hand and once the crowd had quieted, made a short speech about grand gestures of peace and noble sacrifices, and then called us up onto the dais one at a time to put a heavy medal around our necks.

She called me second, and when I bowed in front of her, she murmured, "Well met, granddaughter Gale. Dorothy was a treasure to us, and I have a feeling you will be much the same. Even if you do have an affinity for half-truths." She winked one cat-slitted eye and I felt infinitely better. She knew what had really happened, but she was willing to play the game as I'd laid it out. It was safer for all involved.

We turned to the crowd and Ozma raised her hands. "I present to you, Earthers worthy of Oz!"

The applause was deafening and there was even some cheering. I smiled and curtsied, and then we started to make our way out of the hall as we had been instructed. There was going to be a feast later: all Earther dishes in our honor. I shook hands all the way out, and a young woman carrying a glass cat palmed me a note just as we were exiting the hall. Once the doors had closed, I turned my back to Diggs, who was staring at a tapestry on the wall and drooling, and opened the note.

*Watch your back—they know.*
*— JJ.*

Made in the USA
Columbia, SC
21 August 2018